Home Sweet Home

Published by Advance Publishers, L.C.
www.advance-publishers.com

Written by Holly Melton
Art layout by Niall Harding
Art composition by sheena needham • ess design
Produced by Bumpy Slide Books

ISBN: 1-57973-071-X

Blue's Clues Discovery Series

Hi! It's me, Steve! My puppy Blue and I are making a birdhouse.

BLUE'S BIRD FEEDER

You will need: a cardboard milk or orange juice carton, scissors, glue, pop sticks, paintbrushes, heavy string or fishing line, and non-toxic, washable, acrylic paint

1. Make sure the carton is clean and dry. Ask a grown-up to cut openings on opposite sides of the carton.

2. Glue the pop stick "shingles" onto the roof.

3. Use paints to decorate the carton.

4. To add a perch, ask a grown-up to make a slit in the carton below the openings. Tape pop sticks together for extra thickness, and slip them through the slits.

5. Fill the bottom of your feeder with birdseed.

6. Use heavy string or fishing line to hang your bird feeder from a tree branch. Hang it in the shade so the birds won't get too hot.

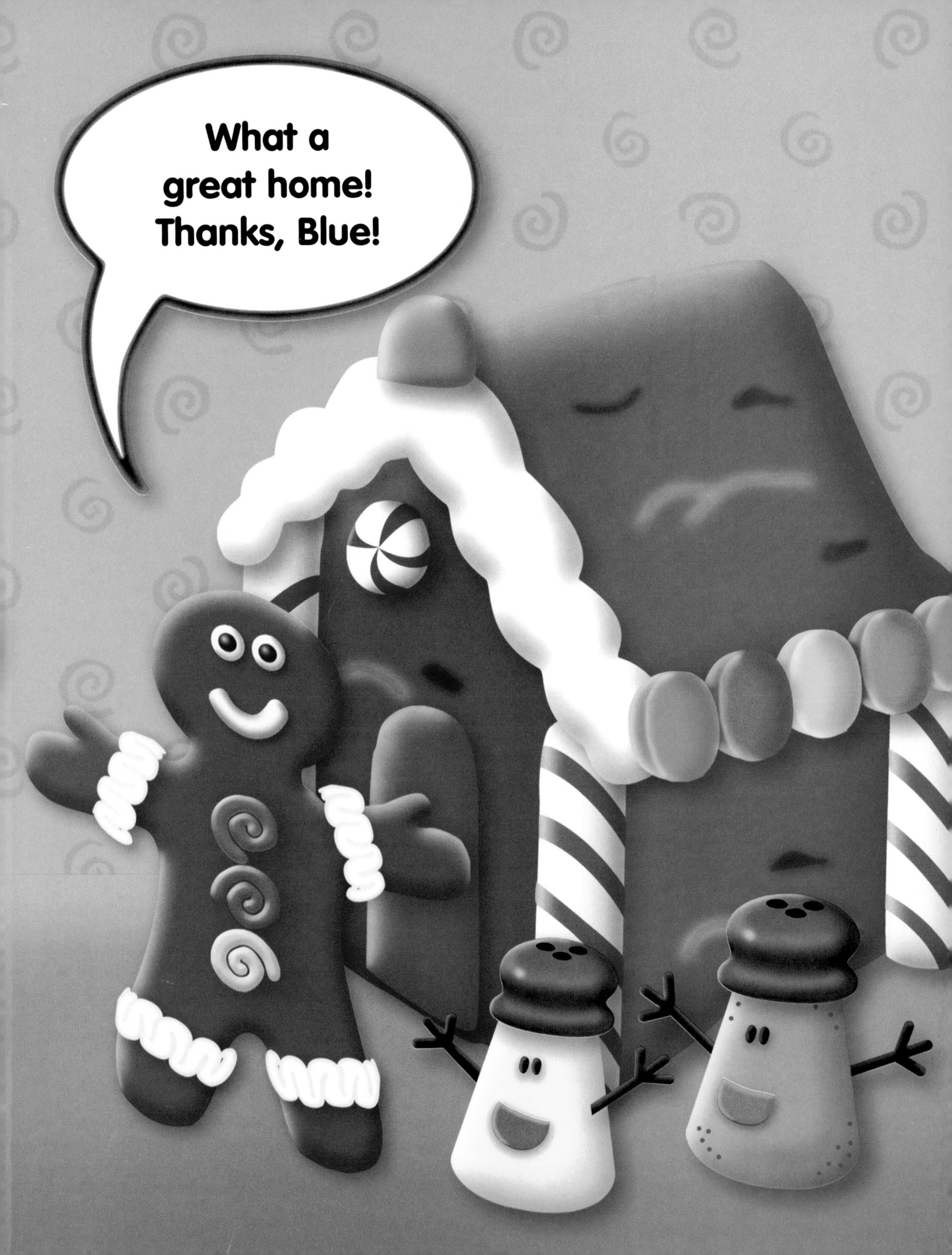
What a great home! Thanks, Blue!

This really is a home, sweet home! It looks like Gingerbread Boy has already moved in! Thanks for all of your help! You did a great job!

Good idea! We can use gingerbread for the walls and the roof, the frosting to hold them together, and the candy to decorate!

We did it! We figured out Blue's Clues!
Blue wants to make a gingerbread house for
Gingerbread Boy! So can you help us find
what we need to make a gingerbread house?

Let's think. So, what kind of home does Blue want to make with a candy cane, gumdrops, and gingerbread? Do you know?

Cool! What's that? You see a clue? Where? Oh! The gingerbread is our third clue! You know where we have to go now? Right! It's time to go to our . . . Thinking Chair! Come on!

We're back! And look who's here. Hi, Gingerbread Boy!
Hi, Steve! Hi, Blue! I was just helping Mr. Salt and Mrs. Pepper.

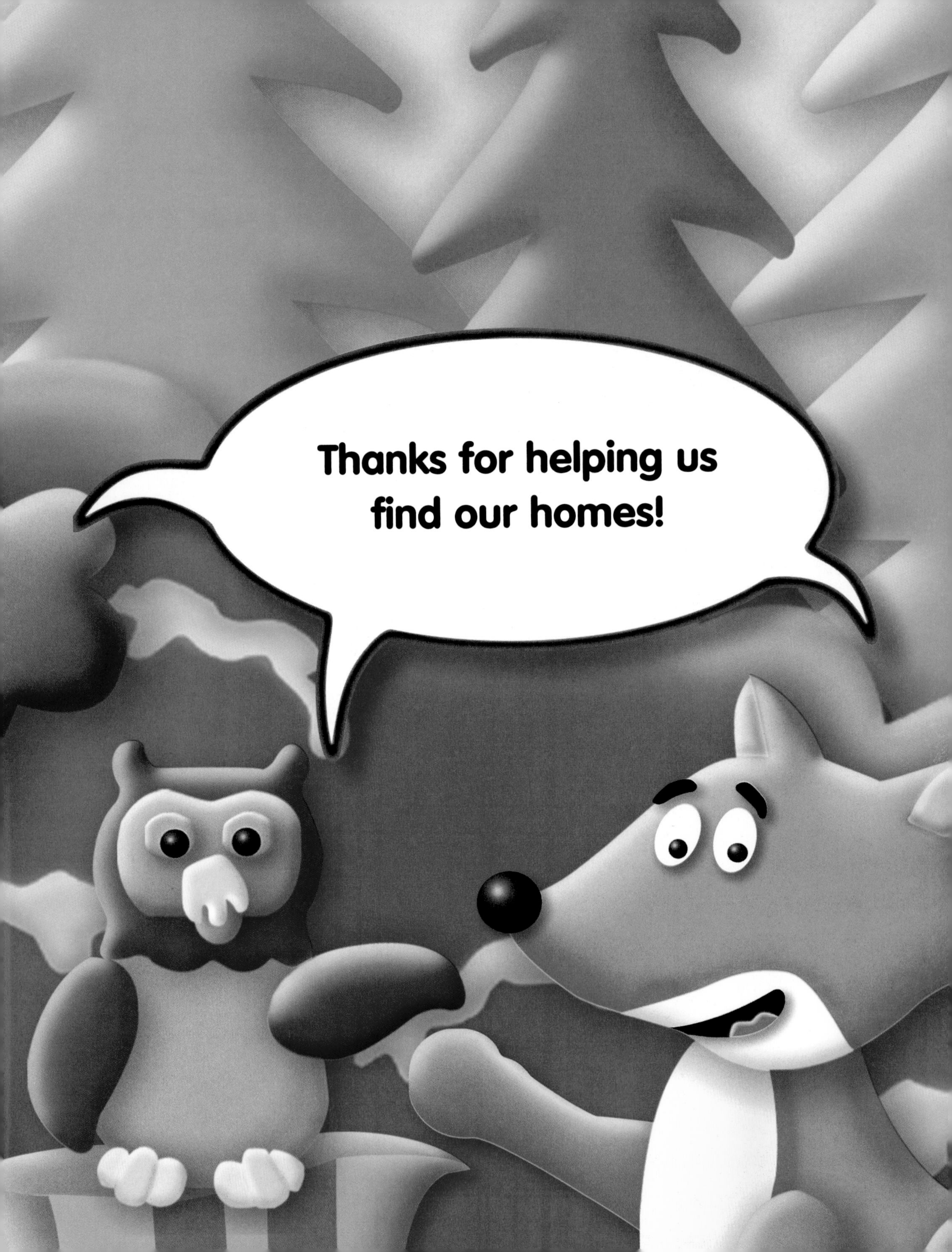
Thanks for helping us find our homes!

Speaking of home, we'd better go back to ours. We still have one more clue to find! Let's go!

You did it! You are a great home finder! Owl found her tree, Fox found his burrow, and Bear found his cave.

Wow! I didn't realize there were so many animal homes in the forest. Do you see any more?

I need to find my home. When it rains, my home is warm and dry.
Can you help me, too? My home is underground.

Oh! Blue Skidoo, we can too!
It looks like Owl, Bear, and
Fox are lost.
Do you see their homes?

Can you help
me find my home?
It's part of a tree.

Hi, Mr. Salt. Hi, Mrs. Pepper. Mmmm, smells good in here! What's that? Do you see a clue? Oh, gumdrops! Gumdrops are our second clue. Great! One more clue to go, right Blue? Blue?

Allo, Allo!
We are cooking up a sweet surprise! Doesn't it smell delicious?
Baking Soda

Hmmm. Water . . . rocks . . . food. Yeah, it looks like Turquoise has everything she needs to feel right at home!

Watching Turquoise eat is making me hungry. C'mon! Let's visit Mr. Salt and Mrs. Pepper's home—otherwise known as the kitchen!

What is that crunching sound? Oh! It's
Blue's turtle, Turquoise, munching on some
lettuce. And she's in her . . . what's the
name of the place where she lives?
That's right! An aquarium!

Sounds like the perfect home for you, Slippery! Hey, let's see if we can find some other homes. See you later, Slippery!

There you are, Blue! Hi, Slippery! What are you doing?

I'm cleaning up! This bathroom is my home, so I like to keep it nice and neat. I slip and I slide all over the place! Whoa!

Look! The Felt Friends have made a home, too. It has a triangle for the roof, square windows, and . . . what is the shape for the door? Oh, yeah! A rectangle! What did you say? You found our first clue? Where? Oh, that candy cane. Good job! Now can you help me find Blue? She went that way? Great! Thanks!

So what kind of home should we make now? Oh, good idea, Blue! We'll play Blue's Clues to figure out what kind of home Blue wants to make next! Will you help? Great! Let's go inside and see what other kinds of homes we can find.

Hi, birds! Make yourselves at home! There's plenty to eat—and a great view, too!

Let's see, what should we do next? Good thinking! We'll finish gluing the roof on. We're almost done. Cool!